for Beth

GIVE US
THIS DAY
THE LORD'S PRAYER

Illustrated by
Tasha Tudor

PHILOMEL BOOKS
New York

Our Father,
who art in heaven,

Hallowed be thy Name,

Thy kingdom come,

Thy will be done,

On earth as it is in heaven.

Give us this day
our daily bread.

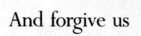

And forgive us
our trespasses,

As we forgive those
who trespass against us.

And lead us not

into temptation,

But deliver us from evil.

For thine is the kingdom,

and the power, and the glory,

for ever and ever.

Amen.

About The Lord's Prayer

The Lord's Prayer comes to us from two Biblical accounts of the words of Jesus: in the Gospel of St. Luke, Chapter 11, verses 2–4, and in the Gospel of St. Matthew, Chapter 6, verses 9–13. Both versions agree in essence, but there are small differences in wording. Matthew's version is the more familiar one, but there are some slight variations in usage, due, probably, to the fact that it has been translated several times and from several sources.

Some readers, for instance, may be more accustomed to the word "debts" than the word "trespasses," which is used in this book. The appearance of the word "trespasses" in the Lord's Prayer is derived from William Tyndale's translation of the Bible into English from Hebrew and Greek originals. Tyndale's was not the first English translation of the Bible, but it was the first English version to be *printed*—it appeared in 1526—and therefore had considerable impact. It was soon followed by several other translations, but it was Tyndale's use of "trespasses" in the Lord's Prayer that was followed in the Book of Common Prayer (1549) of the Church of England, and, in 1789, in the Book of Common Prayer of the Episcopal Church of the United States of America. Roman Catholic churches in English-speaking countries also use this version of the prayer.

But in spite of the small differences in wording that exist, all Christians agree on the essential meaning of this most universal of all prayers. Indeed, the significance of the Lord's Prayer is not restricted to Christians. First formulated by Jesus for His followers, Jews and Gentiles alike, as the proper way for them to address their God, it remains a magnificent expression of faith, that can be valued and loved by all peoples.

About Tasha Tudor

Tasha Tudor is one of America's most distinguished and beloved artists; her illustrations have brought her many honors and awards, and are cherished by both children and adults. Her first book was published in 1938, and since then she has illustrated more than sixty others, many of which she also wrote.

Ms. Tudor lives in southern Vermont in a charming house of her own design, surrounded by her beautiful flower and vegetable gardens and orchards overlooking peaceful meadows and rich woodlands. She shares her home with several corgi dogs, an enormous Irish wolfhound, over two dozen birds, a trio of cats and a pet snake, as well as various temporary residents—farm or woodland creatures that often serve as her models. Several of her children and grandchildren live near enough for frequent visits.

Born in Boston, Ms. Tudor grew up in New England in the countryside she so lovingly portrays in her illustrations. *Give Us This Day: The Lord's Prayer* is a companion volume to her book *The Lord Is My Shepherd: The Twenty-Third Psalm*. Both works express a deeply felt reverence that speaks to both old and young.

Illustrations copyright © 1987 by Tasha Tudor.
Special contents copyright © 1987 by Philomel Books.
Published by Philomel Books, a member of The Putnam Publishing Group,
51 Madison Avenue, New York, NY 10010. All rights reserved.
Published simultaneously in Canada by General Publishing Co., Limited, Toronto.
Design by Nanette Stevenson. Calligraphy by Jeanyee Wong.

Library of Congress Cataloging-in-Publication Data. Lord's prayer. English.
Give us this day. Summary: Presents the text of the most widely known version
of the Lord's prayer, with illustrations and brief commentary on the prayer's
origins and different versions. 1. Lord's prayer—Illustrations—Juvenile literature. [1. Lord's prayer] I. Tudor, Tasha, ill. II. Title. BV232.L6713   1987
226'.96'00222   86-30557 ISBN 0-399-21442-9   First printing